Naptime for Slippers

by **Andrew Clements**
illustrated by **Janie Bynum**

Dutton Children's Books ● **New York**

For Matthew and Tricia Clements,
whose love for their dogs has brought joy and inspiration to so many
A.C.

To Mo, who loves her puppies!
XO, J.B.

Text copyright © 2005 by Andrew Clements
Illustrations copyright © 2005 by Janie Bynum

Library of Congress Cataloging-in-Publication Data
Clements, Andrew, date.
Naptime for Slippers / by Andrew Clements; illustrated by Janie Bynum.— 1st ed. p. cm.
Summary: Slippers the puppy would rather pay attention to interesting smells,
sounds, and sights than take a nap.
ISBN 0-525-47287-8
1. Dogs—Juvenile fiction. [1. Dogs—Fiction. 2. Animals—Infancy—Fiction.
3. Naps(Sleep)—Fiction.] I. Bynum, Janie, ill. II. Title.
PZ10.3.C5937Nap 2004
[E]—dc22 2003027886

Published in the United States by Dutton Children's Books,
a division of Penguin Young Readers Group
345 Hudson Street, New York, New York 10014
www.penguin.com

Designed by Beth Herzog

Manufactured in China
First Edition

1 3 5 7 9 10 8 6 4 2

Slippers had nothing to do.

Daddy was at work.

Mommy was outside.

Laura was at school.

Edward was taking his nap.

So Slippers lay down in his little house.

Then he sat up.

Then he scratched an itch.

Then he lay down again.

Slippers did not like naptime.

Then Slippers heard something.
He tilted his head and perked up one ear.
The hair on his back stood up, and he growled.

Slippers climbed onto a chair
and looked out the window.

It was only Mommy.
She was working in the garden.

Slippers wagged his tail.
He loved to work in the garden.

So Slippers pushed his nose
through the doggy door
and ran outside to help Mommy.

First he pulled up
some red things.

Then he dug up
some orange things.
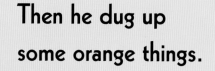

Then he chewed up
some green things.

Then he ate some worms
and some nice soft dirt.

Then Slippers dug a big hole,
and he buried the red things
and the orange things
and the green things.

The garden work made Slippers hot and thirsty.
So he pushed his nose through the doggy door,
and he went across the kitchen,
and he drank all the water from his bowl.

He was still thirsty, so he sniffed.

MILK!

Slippers jumped onto Edward's chair.
Tip, sip, slurp—all gone!

Slippers went back to his little house.
He yawned.

He curled up.
He closed one eye.

Then he closed his other eye.

But then he sniffed.
He opened his eyes and sat up.

He sniffed, and he sniffed,
and his nose said, "It's Edward!"
So Slippers followed his nose.

But it wasn't Edward.
It was just Edward's shoe.
But it smelled very nice—like Edward.

So Slippers took the shoe to his little house.
And he chewed on the shoe,
and he licked the shoe,
and then he buried the shoe under his pillow.

Chewing and licking and burying made him tired,
so Slippers lay down in his little house again.
He yawned. He curled up.
He closed one eye. Then he closed his other eye.

But then Slippers heard something.
Something like this:
drip . . . drip . . . drip.

Slippers ran up the stairs
and into the bathroom.
And there it was, in the tub—
drip . . . drip . . . drip.

So Slippers jumped up and over
and into the tub.

He put out his tongue—
drip . . . drip . . . drip.

But the water was too hot.
So Slippers got out of the tub.
Then he sniffed.
He sniffed, and he sniffed,
and then his nose said, "It's Laura!"

So Slippers followed his nose.

But it wasn't Laura.
It was just Laura's cap.
But it smelled very nice—like Laura.

So Slippers took the cap
all the way back to his little house.

And he chewed on the cap,
and he licked the cap,
and then he buried the cap under his pillow.

Slippers lay down in his little house.
He yawned. He curled up. He closed one eye.
But just before Slippers closed his other eye,
something moved.

21

Slippers sat up. He bent over.
It was a bug.

The bug went fast.
So Slippers followed it.

The bug scurried across the floor
and under the door.

So Slippers pushed his nose
through the doggy door and ran outside.
He went into the garage.

But the bug was gone.

So Slippers sniffed.
He sniffed, and he sniffed,
and then his nose said, "It's Daddy!"
So Slippers followed his nose.

But it wasn't Daddy.
It was just Daddy's work glove.
But it smelled very nice—like Daddy.

So Slippers took the glove
back to his little house.

And he chewed on the glove,
and he licked the glove,

and then he buried the glove under his pillow.

Then Slippers heard Edward.

So did Mommy.
"I'm coming, Edward."
Slippers followed Mommy up the stairs
to Edward's room.

Mommy gave Edward a hug.
"Look who had a good nap!
Let's put on your shoes and take a nice long walk.
And Slippers can come, too."

Edward clapped his hands,
and Slippers wagged his tail.
Slippers loved to take nice long walks.

But not this time.

Slippers went all the way
back to his little house.
He yawned.

He curled up.

He closed one eye.
And then he closed his other eye.

And he did not sniff anything.
And he did not hear anything.
And he did not see anything.

Slippers was ready for naptime.

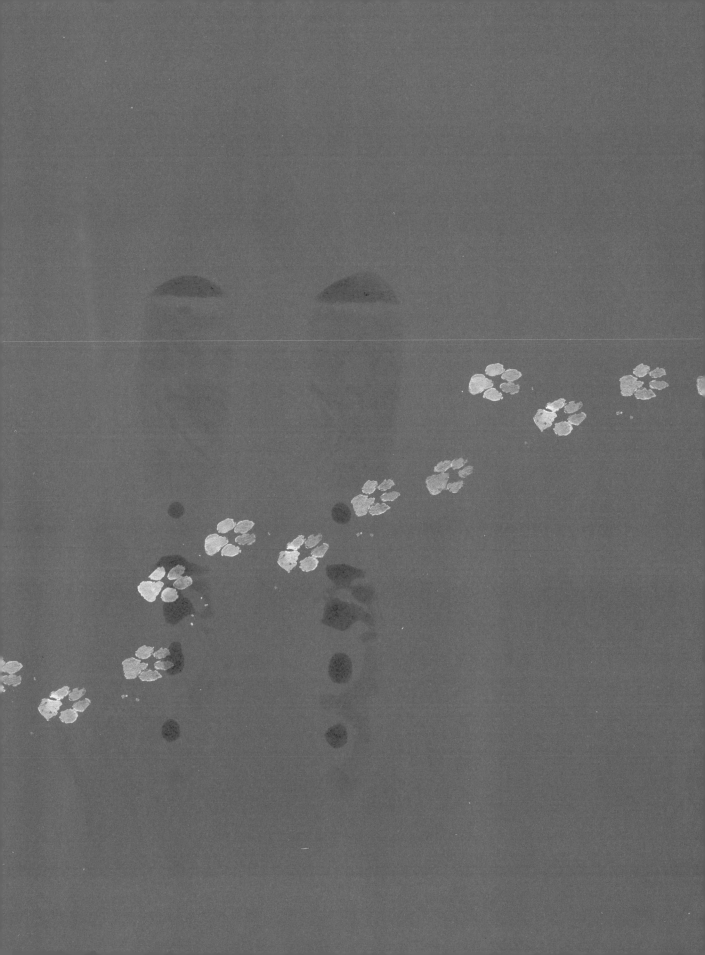